The Selchie's Seed

The Selchie's

Seed

Shulamith Levey Oppenheim

ILLUSTRATED BY

Diane Goode

HARCOURT BRACE & COMPANY

San Diego   New York   London

Requests for permission to make copies of any part of the work should be mailed to:
Permissions Department, Harcourt Brace & Company, 6277 Sea Harbor Drive,
Orlando, Florida 32887-6777.

First Harcourt Brace paperback edition 1996
First published in 1975 by Bradbury Press

Library of Congress Cataloging-in-Publication Data
Oppenheim, Shulamith Levey.
   The selchie's seed/Shulamith Oppenheim; illustrated by Diane
Goode.
     p. cm.
   Summary: Unknowingly descended from a line of seal folk, fifteen-
year-old Marian, living on a remote North Sea island, finds herself
spellbound by a mysterious white whale.
   ISBN 0-15-201412-8
   [1. Supernatural—Fiction. 2. Whales—Fiction. 3. Seals
(Animals)—Fiction. 4. Islands—Fiction.] I. Goode, Diane, ill.
II. Title.
PZ7.O618Se 1996
[Fic]—dc20   96-2279

F E D C B A
Designed by Trina Stahl
Text set in Cloister
Printed in the United States of America

For my children Claire,
Paul, and Daniel,
with love

—S. L. O.

For Peter

—D. G.

"We are, I know not how,
Double in ourselves."

—MONTAIGNE

The Selchie's Seed

*T*HE MERMAID sits upon the rock and laughs. Her eyes are black and her hair is black and the half of her that is of the sea is soft and velvet and gray as the seal. Around the rock swims a white whale, magnificent creature. He plunges and surfaces and plunges again.

The rock lies off a wild isolated group of islets so close by each other they appear to overlap into a single land mass. The water circling the rock like a polished vein of serpentine is leek green. Farther out the sea reflects rich purple laced with foam, and in the distance, ink blue.

It is summer. And with summer comes calm weather and sunshine and the black-backed gulls dipping and rising overhead. The days are warm for only a few months of each year in this part of the North Sea. In winter the sea beats upon the desolate coast, driving the islanders into their cottages of stone and turf, where there is warmth, and blaand to drink—boiling water mixed with buttermilk—delicious on a night of freezing wind and rain. It was on such a night, one bitter cold February two centuries ago, that the white whale and mermaid met for the first time.

Chapter 1

OST OF the fisherfolk lived close by a sheltered landlocked harbor on the south side of the largest island. Edward Sinclare had preferred, for his family, a lonely spit of rock jutting north into the sea. At first view it seemed a barren, treacherous site, where no tree, not even the creeping willow, might find soil enough to root and thrive. But just below the cottage ran a fertile green strath, a little valley that paralleled the bottomless voe beside the house. Many natives caught the seal, the selchie, in such narrow arms of the sea where the creatures became entangled in nets. The Sinclares never hunted the seal. They shied away from anything to do with it, the wearing of its skin, the eating of its flesh. Edward Sinclare harvested the haafbanks far off-shore for cod and ling and halibut and herring. The sea was kind to him, even when others had a poor catch. Toward every rich pocket of fish he waved the others on, and all shared.

One son, sixteen, fished with his father and a crew. One daughter kept the household with her mother. Already, at fifteen, the girl had been spoken for many times, her hand asked in marriage by the young fishermen of the village, by the neighbor who helped man the sixareen, the six-oared clinker boat, and by the young schoolmaster. Perhaps one of them might have won her, if what happened had not happened the night of the storm.

Just after dark that night, Edward Sinclare and his son shook water from their broad-brimmed hats and pulled open the cottage door that fought against them, so strong was the wind.

The older man drew off his boots and cape and strode into the main room of the cottage. Graeme followed. Most islanders bore Scots names, but often the blood ran pure Norse. Father and son were blue eyed and fair haired and massive.

"I've had you with me during many a storm, but I've never felt so close to not returning. Where's Marian?" Edward called for his daughter. "Where's my girl?"

"She's gone to find the pony and put him in the byre," his wife answered from the back bedclosets.

"She left only a few minutes ago—with such a gale as I hear!"

Ursilla Sinclare came into the room and drew her husband and son to the fire.

She smiled. "I must tell you. I'm glad you're back. You're both bone wet. Get out of those clothes and drink some blaand. Just mixed."

Ursilla had come from the Hebrides as a bride. She was taller than ordinary, long limbed, long fingered, with beautiful hands that seemed slung from her wrists. Her hair was raven and her eyes were dark and deep as the coves and caves. Ursilla's was a beautiful face, open and generous. And generous she was, with her talent for healing. What little was known of her past life was never questioned, for her kindnesses were enough to make her admired by all. She once treated the entire settlement during the smallpox epidemic that had threatened from Mainland. An incision on the upper arm, a bit of peat-dried dung under the skin, a cabbage leaf for a bandage. And not a one had died.

But it was Marian whom the islanders had taken to their hearts. It was Marian's winning voice and gentle ways and milk-white skin abloom on each cheek that made them smile when they saw her and smile when they thought of her. It was Marian with her blush and black-fringed eyes that caused the young men of the island to lose their breath and

give up their hearts at the turning of her fifteenth summer, when the weather was fairest.

Now the weather was at its worst. Edward drank up and started for the door.

"It's not a night for Marian to be out, Ursilla, pony or no. I'll get her. It's not a night for a young girl to be wandering loch and cliff. The wind has force enough to fling down a body ten times her size."

"Let me go, Father." Graeme pulled on his cape that was still hanging from one shoulder. "I've searched out that pony before. He's a cunning one. He thrives on such a night."

The boy was gone before his father could stop him.

Chapter 2

ONCE OUTSIDE, Graeme headed for the path behind the cottage that led to the strath. There were no roof gutters, and the water sluiced down as from an overturned bucket. He passed the byre where the animals were sheltered. No sign of his sister. The rain was now a drenching sheet on all sides of him, and the wind lashed out in a fury.

"Marian, hooohooo, Marian!" Graeme shouted against the storm. "I can't see my feet, let alone that sister of mine," he muttered to himself. "Best get a lantern."

Turning back, he stood peering into the churning black water of the voe. At that moment, the wind split the curtain of rain and he caught sight of a form doubled over at the bottom of the rocky descent.

Graeme ran diagonally down the precipitous drop. Dangerous at all times, the small jagged rocks that spiked out of the cliff were killers in such a tempest. As he neared the bottom, he bent his knees to catch his own weight and landed beside his sister.

She was staring into the water, shivering. Graeme grabbed her arm and pulled her to him. For into the boiling inlet had either swum or been forced a huge sea creature. Through the darkness he could just make out a transparency of skin. At intervals the body convulsed, the fluke thrashed from side to side.

Brother and sister were level with its beak—for the creature had a kind of beak and had turned its head to look at Marian. The girl did not move.

"Marian! *Marian! Come away.*" Graeme spoke close to his sister's ear. Her head was swathed in a scarf over which she had drawn the same kind of hat he was wearing. "What *is* it, what's the matter?"

She made no reply.

"It's bitter cold. You're shivering. Marian?"

The girl was trying to shake free of her brother's hold. She pulled on him and leaned low over the creature's head. Graeme wrenched her back.

"Marian, for the Lord's sake, what's got you? Don't put your face near it!" By now he was screaming.

Suddenly Marian turned her face to his.

"Graeme, I don't know what it is. I came because of the bells. I was putting Jo into the byre—he'd been in the winter garden eating the kale. I followed the sound, clear as Sunday," the girl paused, "and I found him. He's hurt. His flipper is torn. It was above water when I first came. He's in pain, Graeme," and she buried her head on her brother's soaking chest. The boy held her sobbing against him.

The creature was no longer convulsing. Its head was raised higher out of the water and its eye—there was no mistaking—its eye held an intelligence. It was no fish eye, this. Graeme could see that. But this was not the moment to think about it. He had to get Marian back to the cottage. The girl was still clinging to his cape.

Graeme looked up, for the storm had suddenly abated. Across the inlet he saw coming toward them flickering sweeps of light. It was the aurora after a gale. He had only seen it once before, as a very small child. It threw eerie shimmers on the rock surfaces and at the same time made it possible for the two to see more clearly whatever was in the water beside them. Marian turned from her brother, and with a little cry knelt close to the creature. Graeme sucked in his breath.

"Oh, Marian! Such a thing! Here! A white whale!"

Marian had become, in an insant, calm. She stretched out a hand toward the whale.

"Lovely creature." Her voice was itself like a bell. Then even more softly, again, "Lovely creature."

Graeme started, not at his sister's words, but at the movement of the whale. It had immersed its head in the water and then brought it high up, its short beak slightly parted.

"There, Graeme. You heard them this time, the bells?"

Her brother had heard nothing. "Silly goose! I didn't hear anything. And besides, how do you know it's a *he?*"

"Oh, Graeme!" The girl's words were liquid and her face was transparent with light. It could have been made of glass. "Oh, Graeme, *I know.*"

"All right. All right. But you've been out long enough and so have I, and Mother and Father will be worrying, Father especially. Let's go."

Graeme raised Marian to her feet and away from the gaze of the whale. The girl resisted. "The whale needs me close by him—his flipper is torn, he is in pain," she said. "He mustn't be alone." Her words were full of tenderness and her face, turned toward the creature, was full of longing, gentle.

What Graeme read in the whale's eye, glancing back as he guided his sister steadily up the near-vertical incline before him, was determined and un-wavering: a creature within his rights, his rights to fill the sea arm beside their cottage that night.

As the two disappeared, the whale gave a mighty thrash with his fluke that sent the waters rolling in great swells against the side of the voe.

Chapter 3

BY THE TIME they reached the cottage it was as if the storm had never been. Stars winked through space and a scimitar moon had risen. There was no wind. Only the sea continued to churn, as the heart keeps racing even after danger has passed.

"I'll be fine now, thank you," Marian said as she slipped away from Graeme's guiding hands. "I don't know what happened. I couldn't have lifted a foot from the ground. You're a good brother."

Then, just as he reached out to pull open the door, Marian stopped Graeme.

"Don't tell Mother and Father I cried, please. We'll tell them about the whale and Mother will go down with the salve. Just say—"

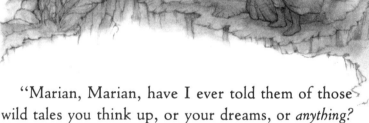

"Marian, Marian, have I ever told them of those wild tales you think up, or your dreams, or *anything?* Don't worry." He opened the door and the two went in.

The table was set with wooden plates and utensils. In the center stood a steaming kettle of potatoes and fish. Their parents were already eating. Edward looked up and grinned.

"Well, that's better. From the time you two have been gone, I'll guess you've given your brother one merry chase." He wiped his mouth on a piece of worsted. "So come over here and give your father one merry hug."

Marian threw herself onto her father. Edward howled. "Ho! Those cheeks and hands are ice, girl!"

Ursilla waved them toward their bedclosets.

"Out of those clothes, both of you. Supper will stay hot. I've enough illness to care for this winter without my own falling sick."

A short time later they were eating quietly, breaking up bits of bread into the golden broth. Edward asked, "Any trouble finding Jo?"

Graeme answered quickly. "You know that pony, Father. It took time, but he's snug in now. Marian's sure he's a nuggle, a mysterious creature come from the lochs, or rather," and he flashed a grin at his sister, "she *hopes* he's a nuggle."

Marian gave Graeme a solid kick under the table. They continued eating in silence, but Marian was bursting. She shoved her brother's foot again, this time in tiny nudges, as if urging him on. She knew he would know how to bring it up, and he would probably say . . .

"Father, when last did anyone sight a white whale around here?"

Edward put down his spoon. "Maybe forty year, maybe longer. They come down from the north, a sight to see!"

"Have you ever seen one?" Marian asked as calmly as she could.

"I'll say I did. I was nearing five, maybe younger. One stranded on Whalsay. We took ship to have a look."

"No," Marian insisted, "I mean *live*, in the water." *Why,* thought the girl, *is Mother looking like that?*

"Live? No. No, never. But this one I did see measured fourteen feet. Most times they run, well, eight feet, maybe nine. Pure white. When they're full grown, they're pure white. They yellow with age. They've a sound comes from them, like bells. Not all human folk hear it. Sea canaries, that's what they're called, for the bells."

Marian did not look at Graeme. She lowered her head over her bowl. Ursilla lifted the kettle from the table onto a sideboard by the washing bucket. She came back and stood between the two children, a hand resting with its own peculiar grace on each.

"I know my son and daughter," she said. "Why all the questions about a white whale?"

Graeme put his hand over his mother's. His was broad with thick fingers, but hers tapered beyond his at least an inch, if not more. The boy knew he would have to tell it.

"There's a white whale in the voe, caught—well, not caught—but it has torn a flipper and it's just lying there."

Marian grabbed her mother's skirt. "And he's in pain, Mother, he told—" She stopped short. "I mean he's *surely* in pain, he'd have to be . . . He's really beautiful, Father." Her eyes were pleading as she looked at her parents and added, "You'll put the salve on the flipper, won't you, Mother? Tonight?"

The girl's face was flushed. Ursilla looked at her husband. Edward was already walking to the door.

"Clean up for your mother, *both* of you. Ursilla, get what you'll need, and your heaviest shawl. I

think the storm's past, but I'll wager the air cuts to the bone.''

Without a word, his wife gathered up a thick, closely knit green shawl from the back of her chair and went to a tiny cupboard by the far door. She came away with a rather large wooden jar and a piece of finely woven cloth. In a moment only Marian and Graeme were left.

"It's all right now, Marian. You'll see, Mother will put on the salve, and Father will know if there's anything else amiss. And tomorrow we'll go down at sunup to see how it's faring. *If* it's still there.''

Marian had started clearing the table. She stopped midway to the sideboard.

"He'll be there, Graeme. He's not *stranded*. You know that! He'll be there.''

Chapter 4

URSILLA AND Edward stood looking down at the white whale. The creature lay high on the water, with the flipper exposed. Ursilla knelt and took the cover from the salve pot. The whale watched intently her every move. She lifted up the flipper. It had indeed been ripped. The flesh was sheared, but the bleeding had stopped. Edward dropped to his knees beside his wife and took the fleshy forepart from her. She pulled the strip of cloth from beneath her shawl and scooped up a dab of the milky salve: nettle juice, pounded bramble leaves, and sheep's fat, whipped to a cream. With light, short strokes she covered the gash. Edward laid the flipper down. It remained above water.

"Soon mended," he said, patting his wife's arm.

"A white whale! It's a sight to see!" Then, "You're trembling, Ursilla. The cold has come through that shawl. We'll go back now."

His wife hesitated. Something had rooted her there.

"Edward, I'd like another look at the flipper."

"But you've just put on the salve. Such a wound will need days to heal."

"I still want another look. Please, Edward."

Ursilla knelt again. With the same cloth, she wiped away the salve that she had applied only moments before. There was no gash, no tear. Not a trace. Not a line nor a scar. Ursilla could feel the eye of the whale upon her, but she dared not look back. Edward stared in disbelief. Then he looked at his wife, and a cold tremor shot through him.

Marian was sitting quietly, hands folded, when her parents returned.

"Your mother put on the salve. The whale will soon be well and off." Edward looked straight at Graeme, though his words were for Marian. The girl knew her parents. No more would be said that evening.

Marian pulled a soft flannel nightdress over her shivering form. In body she was like her mother, only finer boned and slimmer. Her movements were fluid. Graeme said she flowed rather than walked, and when she talked, she swept the words along with her hands.

The pillow still smelled bittersweet, of the herbs her mother had packed into its center when she was a bride, years before. The sheets were of a thinner flannel, and like the heavy blanket, had been woven and sewn at home, by Ursilla and herself.

The girl moved deep into the comfort of the bed. And then, like the shock of a noise just as sleep drifts in, a pain cut through the warmth, a pain of fright making her grip the side of the box bed.

Marian pressed her face into the pillow.

"Lord, what's happening to me? Oh, please, what is it? White he is, pure white. Beautiful he is. Can it be that he is so beautiful?"

She uttered a piercing little cry, from far within her; she lifted her face from the pillow, and her hand flew to her mouth, as if to push the cry inward. Graeme stirred in the bedcloset just beyond.

"I can't breathe." Marian sat bolt upright. *"I can't breathe!* I was all right. When we came back to the house and Father talked about the whales. Lord, he *is* a whale. I know it . . . as well as I know who I am and that Jo's a pony but—" The girl buried her face in the pillow again. "I told Graeme he's not stranded. He'll be there."

Where a few moments before her limbs ached with cold, the sweat now was drawing the flannel to her skin. Her heart was pounding and skipping beats at the same time. It was as if she were going to scream or lose breath or both.

"I'll wake Graeme. No! I'll think. Help me to think it out. Please, Lord."

Marian forced herself down under the covers.

From the icy depths of a polar midnight this sea creature had come, his body fatted with her dreams, stored under the sleekness of his skin, but most of all, burning from the jet of his eye. . . .

Marian pushed herself lower and lower into the bed, until she was curled in a ball, her slender legs pulled up against her chest, her arms encircling her knees. She began rocking back and forth. Ever so slowly the panic eased.

"Tomorrow I'll go down and see him. When it's light. It's a new world in daylight. I'll be calm."

Marian pulled her legs tighter to her body. Soon she slept.

In the voe, the white whale idled at the surface of the water. His paddle-shaped flippers hung loosely, his fluke rigid and taut. Through the blowhole on the top of his globelike head, he drew long draughts of air into his enormous lungs. *He* would not sleep this night.

Chapter 5

MORNING BROUGHT sun and a knife-edged wind. Marian gulped down the oatmeal porridge her mother had set out. She got up from the table and embraced Ursilla, then stood away at arm's length. She would be calm!

"Mother, you didn't say a word last night when you came back. We could see you were tired. But isn't he glorious? Did he mind when you put on the salve?"

There it was again, that look of such alarm on her mother's face.

The fear is mine and mine alone, Ursilla had repeated to herself through a tormented night. *The fear has always been mine, and the waiting.*

"Mother?"

Ursilla forced a smile. "Surely, child, it is a grand whale. Your father thinks it will be healed quickly and soon off. Such a one does not linger near human kind. We'll see it off soon, very soon."

No, foolish woman. Ursilla watched the shadow cross and be gone from Marian's glowing face. *No, Ursilla Sinclare, you know these words have no power. What is now come, is come. What is, is.*

"I'm going down to him, Mother. There's time before milking and Jo can wander a bit." And Marian was out the door, her shawl flying behind her.

Through the window Ursilla watched her child skip away toward the rocky descent.

Outside Marian found the ground scattered with white patches. A dozen hardy little sheep were grazing on the strath.

"I hope Graeme has been to see the whale." Marian hummed to herself. Oh yes, she did feel calm. It would be all right. The sun was out. A group of noisy starlings hopped about in the middle of the turf. The air was crisp and, for the girl, full of promise.

With what difficulty she and Graeme had climbed this drop the night before!

Of course the whale would be there!

As Marian approached the voe, the empty water began to stir. First, the blowhole announced his presence with a jet of damp, moist air. Then the long, gleaming back of the whale broke surface, as his head and blowhole submerged in an arc downward. Then the fluke, and finally the whole form, as if feather light, lay extended alongside the rocky edge.

The girl settled down on a strip of rock and clapped her hands.

"Of course you're here!"

The creature rolled over, dashing spray onto Marian, who threw back her head for sheer joy. How could she have felt so ill last night? The whale rolled onto his back and opened his beak.

"Oh, you *are* a glory, and it is a most beautiful day. Your *first* morning here."

Heaving toward the girl, the whale brought his left side almost onto the land. The flipper lay at Marian's feet. She dropped onto her knees and with a finger traced the skin. Then she looked directly into the eye of the whale, which, as the night before, had not taken its gaze from her.

"Why, there's nothing here! Nothing! I can't even tell where the wound was. It's healed!" Marian was standing now and shaking her head. "You're very lucky, you know. Mother does have powers."

Suddenly she was down again, her cheek stroking the brilliant whiteness of the whale's head.

"And I am most lucky of all, that you are here. *So* lucky, I don't even mind the ache your coming has put into my heart."

Marian was barely whispering. Her eyes were

brimming over, and the salt tears mingled freely with the sea. Neither girl nor whale stirred. Then she stood up and without a look back climbed, as quickly as the rough terrain would allow her, up to the cottage and over to the byre.

On the end of the whale's beak, a teardrop had become crystal. It caught the pink of the rising sun and the steel blue of the sand beneath. The whale twisted his head as if testing the jewel's balance against his own.

Then whale and teardrop disappeared below.

Chapter 6

THOSE FISHING the inshore waters sighted the whale early this morning." Graeme handed his father a bundle he had brought him from the village.

"Well they might, it's big enough." Edward began untying the string.

"I told them it had been with us last night, and about the ripped flipper. No one will bother it, for all the stir."

"Don't be expecting to see it around much longer, son. Such a one doesn't swim the skerries when it's got the arctic waters to play in." Edward put his arm about Graeme's shoulder. "Call Marian. I saw her on that pony down by the sheep. It's about time," and Edward looked up at the sun, "it's about time dinner be on the table."

Marian was tethering the pony beside a dark brown ewe whose woolly sides sparkled with chips of ice.

"Jo and Goudie love each other," Marian said. She stroked the pony's nose, then gave the ewe's ear a loving tweak. "Did you see the whale?"

Graeme nodded.

"Then tell me." His sister tucked her arm into his. "*Tell* me, Graeme."

"Tell you what, Marian?"

"What you think. Oh, Graeme, I must talk to someone, my heart cannot carry it alone." She moved almost directly in front of him.

"You, Graeme, you have not always understood the two of me, inside," she put her hands to her cheeks, "so different. But when I'd tell you one *had* to burst out and soar, you would always say—"

"I know what I would say, goose. I would say girls marry and leave home and that's the truth of it, Marian. That's the life happening all about us, and will to you and me. But the other—the dreams and the stories created from them—they will go, they will have to go, Marian, together with the games we've played and the tales we've made up together . . ." The boy's voice grew low. "It's a whale down there in the voe, a white whale probably eight, nine feet long, with a fluke and flippers and fish eyes," he paused, "and a belly full of half-eaten cuttles. A *whale,* Marian."

They were going toward the cottage. Graeme still held his sister's hands while she walked backward, to see his face as they talked.

"Dearest Graeme, I know. But, Graeme," the girl stopped short, "when I think of him, there's not air enough for me to breathe, and my throat closes and I weep. Tell me, Graeme," and she smiled like an embarrassed child, "is he not a *glorious* whale?"

They were at the cottage door. The window was slightly open. Ursilla often pushed out a tiny pane to let the cooking smoke escape. Their father's throaty voice cut through the midday silence.

"I don't believe it, Ursilla. 'Tis not Christian. Pagan it is, not Christian. Superstition! Children of the Seal, the Clan MacCodrum. It be believed, and this I harken to, all seals come from human kind, far far back, and 'tis the reason I kill no seal . . . but the Clan MacCodrum. Descendants! No. *No!*"

Marian and Graeme moved closer to the side of the cottage that made an angle with the window. They pressed themselves flat against the wall, just as their mother's steady voice replied.

"Edward, you saw the flipper. *Kind speaks to kind,* and so it healed. It is not fairy lore that the Clan MacCodrum is directly come from the selchie and all carry within themselves the seed. And now . . ."

"And now . . ." Edward's voice banged as his fist banged the table, "and now, Christian that I am, that you are, you ask me to believe that in my own daughter the seed has rooted and . . ."

Ursilla broke in, *"And will flower.* That is correct. And Edward, I will tell you more. The whale is a finn—a creature of such magic it takes on any form it wishes and takes away anything it desires. Edward," Ursilla's voice gentled, "Edward, when

Marian was born, recall the skin between her fingers and toes? There is little to see now, but . . ."

Outside, brother and sister were stone still. Marian lifted a hand, spread wide as a delicate fan. There, at the base of each finger, fine as dragonfly's wing, were strung tiny bits of transparent skin. Graeme stared at her fingers, then at her face, then back again at her hand. Keeping his own hands close by his sides, he felt about with his thumb at the base of each finger. Nothing there.

"No, Graeme," his sister said, "there is nothing between your fingers. Often I have looked." He let out a long breath. Marian's voice came to him as if from far away. "I never asked after mine. Somehow, I always knew."

Chapter 7

MARIAN COVERED her mouth with a hand.

"Come," Graeme urged, "come, we must go in."

Love, and a dread born of the unknown, raged within the boy. He must give strength to his sister.

Together they entered the cottage.

Their parents were already seated at the table. Instead of a steaming kettle, a long, boat-shaped wooden serving tray held quarters of boiled chicken and mounds of kale. There was no smile from Edward. Ursilla barely looked at her children.

The two sat down and took food from the tray. At one point Edward glanced at Marian as she held out a mug for blaand.

Graeme was nearest the pitcher. He filled his sister's cup, then asked, "Father?"

Edward shook his head.

Graeme, watching Marian, noticed that her face, usually rosy from the cold, was ashen, and she picked at her food. Suddenly she let the spoon clatter onto her dish, took up her shawl, and shot away from the table and the cottage.

No one spoke.

Finally it was Graeme who said, "We heard you talking through the window."

Edward pushed away from the table, a hand clenching each arm of his chair.

"Best she knows. Best she sees the folly of it. She's a sensible girl. She's God-fearing. She's of a Christian family."

Graeme leaned over toward his mother. "What *has* happened, Mother? Is Marian bewitched by the whale?"

Ursilla reached out and patted her son's hand. "If you mean an enchantment, a spell cast upon her, no, Graeme, your sister is not bewitched. The seed of the selchie has always been within her and—"

"The seed of the selchie be damned!" Edward had risen and was fumbling with his cape on the back of his chair. It had caught under a leg when he'd pushed from the table.

"There's a way of being rid of this damnable curse! Selchie I've never killed, but whale shan't trouble me."

Ursilla's hand closed over her son's, and he felt the nails in his flesh. The boy was instantly beside his father.

"Father, you can't! You know you can't, because if you do, Marian will . . ."

By then Ursilla had come to her husband. She lifted the chair, freeing the end of the cape. Her voice was all gentleness and compassion. "Edward. Nothing will change the future. Of what it shall be, I have no more knowledge than you. What I do know is, there is nothing to be done against it."

And she touched Edward's shoulder. The gesture was enough. The father stood weeping. "Our child, Ursilla, dear God!"

Graeme felt tears rise in his own eyes. *What is this they fear?*

It was not ten minutes later that Marian rushed back into the room, as much joy shining through her eyes now as there had been grief when she left. Had she brought the sun into the cottage, it could not have been brighter, for blazing on her shawl was a necklace. The pearls were each as big as a cockle-shell and the coral rounds as smooth as water-worn

pebbles. At the end of the pearl and coral chain hung a crystal teardrop.

"The whale gave it to me!" she said.

"She's mad!" Edward turned to his wife, the blue of his eyes almost black with rage. His fingers worked violently one against the other.

Graeme strode to the door next to his sister. Staring in disbelief at her father, Marian took hold of her brother's arm to steady herself. The words cut through her soul and instantly brought back the fears of the night before—the fears and panic and sickness that in the sunlight had melted away, and that she had been sure would be gone forever when she put the whale's offering about her neck.

"Father . . ." Marian wept the word.

"Stop, girl! Honor thy father and thy mother, that thy days may be long upon the earth! *I* call it madness, that, that . . ." and he pointed to the crystal on Marian's breast. As if answering his ranting, the jewel glowed more brilliantly. "That piece of profanity! Where's the gold cross put on you by your mother and myself when you were born? Where is it, for that creature to see? Then it will know it has no business in these parts, among honest, hard-working Christians!"

Marian fumbled beneath her blouse and pulled out the tiny gold symbol.

"Here, Father, I have never taken it off. Nor would I!"

"Well, let's thank God for that!" Edward fairly bellowed at his daughter. "Where do you think it came from, girl, that king's ransom?"

"Father!" It was Graeme who spoke. "You *know* we honor you. But *you* believe in the Blue Men. What about them? We throw them silver that they may leave our boat in peace. You've told me you've never seen them, yet never do we make the journey to the farthest haafbanks without gifting them with silver. Marian and I heard Mother—the whale is a finn creature, come to be near us for Mother's healing. It was injured and Mother helped it. So it's given Marian the necklace, in thanks. That makes sense, Father." *Please dear God,* Graeme added to himself, *let it make sense.*

"It does not make *my* kind of sense, Graeme," Edward rumbled out. "Other fishermen *have* seen the Blue Men. Blue faced, blue haired they are, all man down to the waist, and fish below. It's always been done, the gifting. It's not the same and . . ." Edward confronted his wife. "You know it, Ursilla. Now *I've* done and I'm leaving to make repairs. Graeme, you're coming with me."

Edward wrenched his cape from the back of the resting chair and went to the door.

"Get your cape, son. We've thatching to do and peat blocks to bring up. Whale or no, the nights are bitter still."

"Go with your father, Graeme." Ursilla's voice was balm on the slashings left by Edward's words. "Marian will stay with me. We've mending and washing . . . and talking."

Fathoms deep, the white whale moved slowly along the seabed, searching. He had no interest in the fish that swam above him. They sensed this, darting closer and ever closer, around and about his gliding body. He cared even less for the crustaceans and crabs that made up his daily food.

With his short beak, he stirred up the sandy bottom, sending strange little forms scurrying out from their homes, troubling and disturbing the plants that swayed frantically in his wake.

From time to time he made joyous sounds like the curlew's song in spring, and with each sound he thrust up from the bottom an object that flamed in the murky water. Soon the whale had left a trail of light behind him, from one end of the voe to the other.

Using his beak, he pushed his treasures together, till at the very end of the inlet, where the sea arm met the sea itself, there was a store of six shells, lying one against the other, strange sheens on indiscernible shapes. Emitting a long cry, the whale rose to the surface of the water—and languished there.

"It's time, isn't it, Mother? That is really why the whale is here—because it's time."

Ursilla touched her daughter's cheek with the back of her hand.

"It is time, my dearest child." Then, not as an afterthought but deliberately spoken, she added, "Perhaps we must say it is time *because* the whale has come. Sit down."

Marian sat by the hearth, Ursilla in a chair beside her. The girl tucked her legs under her skirt and folded her hands in her lap.

"You have heard the legend of the selchie, as we of the islands call the seal. That it was once human and that, when no one is about, it comes ashore and leaves off its skin and takes on human form. Many, many tales have been told about such adventures. One legend has it that a man of the Clan MacCodrum—I was born MacCodrum, this you also know—in a time too far back to measure, came upon the selchies leaving off their skins, about to dance upon the sands at midnight. He stole a skin and hid it away above his door. Soon there came a lovely young girl wandering, distracted, searching for her covering, for without it she could never return to the sea. On sight, this man fell desperately in love with her. They married, for she had no other choice. Numerous children they had, and their life was tranquil, but the girl never ceased pining for the lost sealskin and for the sea. Then one day, many years later, she discovered it, still hidden above the door. Without a word, and never looking back, she put it on and swam away. All her descendants, all those of the Clan MacCodrum, so it is said, have within themselves the selchie's seed. And so it is."

Marian had laid her head upon her mother's knees during the telling, and now she felt a tremor pass through Ursilla's body. She looked up. And Ursilla saw that the girl had grown more beautiful in the last hours, that she was luminous, as if she might become one with light and shadow at any moment.

"Mother, do you know what will happen?"

"I only know what I feel."

"And what is that, Mother?"

"That the magic has come."

"And why to me?"

"That is the magic."

Chapter 8

A WEEK PASSED, the first week of the whale.

Marian had by her bed six shells—all of exotic beauty, all like no shells the Sinclares had ever seen. Each day the girl rose with the sun and ran down to the voe, where she sat for an hour, chattering merrily, sometimes singing the same songs Ursilla had sung to her as a small child, sometimes not saying a word, looking at the whale as he gazed back at her.

When Marian returned to the cottage each day, the whale moved backward from the inlet and out to sea. There, throughout the day, he swam toward and away from land, always in line with the spit of rock, always in crescent-shaped runs, as if enclosing Marian's world in a watery boundary. On the land

above, Marian contrived, despite her chores, to stay within his sight. Only when she rode Jo into the village or looked to the sheep on the strath were they parted from view.

Ursilla watched it all. She watched the graceful, precise dives as the whale marked out his territory and as he moved like an arrow into the voe each evening.

The whale was a common sight now. He was called Sinclare's whale and no one thought otherwise.

On the seventh night, when Graeme and Marian were asleep, Ursilla sat by the fireside working a hapshawl of finest Shetland wool. Edward came and sat beside her. His hands were pushed under his belt.

"May I talk a bit to you, Ursilla?" he asked gravely. "Have you the time?"

"Where shall I be off to this night, Edward, that I would not have the time?" Ursilla looked up at him and laid down her needles. "But first, shut the door to the children's bedclosets."

When it was done, Edward stirred the fire, then drew up a chair opposite his wife.

" 'Tis not been an easy week."

Ursilla nodded.

" 'Tis been quiet, but 'tis been the soul's labor to keep it so."

"Knowing you as I do, Edward, there's truth in that!" Ursilla knew what it had taken for him to let the days pass and the time flow through him, what it had taken for him to keep peace.

Edward was speaking again, the words coming with difficulty.

"You've always spoken out your heart and mind to me, especially when my mind and heart were battling. So I'll ask it straight out. I've a question ringing in my head these last days . . ." It was clear to Ursilla, Edward's voice was filling with pain. "Watching our boy's face by my side in the boat, and looking on our girl. So I'll ask you, Ursilla MacCodrum, what *might* you know that would save us?"

The look he gave her wrung Ursilla's heart. She thought of the whale. It would be relentless, this finn creature.

"Save *us,* my husband? This is wrong thinking. Whatever saves us, as you put it, might bring harm to Marian. There is no stopping magic."

"Harm her by keeping her safe? Ursilla, there's less sense in that than Graeme's excuse for the necklace she keeps about her throat. Try . . . tell more of the selchie. Perhaps in the telling, we will find something."

"So many tales there are, Edward. And many you know. But there's a line through all," she paused, "that when the selchie sheds its skin—some say each night, some say only when the tide makes a certain line with the shore, some say every seventh year— the selchie cannot return to the sea without it . . . ever."

"And the Clan MacCodrum—there's no doubt, Ursilla? *No* doubt?"

Ursilla shook her head. "No doubt. My great-grandmother, from whom came my wedding trunk, she more than anyone would writhe in pain during the yearly seal hunt."

Edward was staring into the fire.

"And what of that finn creature, that white whale in the voe?"

Ursilla stretched out her hands and took Edward's to her breast. A weariness was coming over her. "It is too strong for us, Edward, it is too strong."

Edward would not be put off.

"There are charms, Ursilla. You, with your power of healing . . . there are charms and herbs for every sickness—and this may be a sickness."

Her poor Edward. "There are no charms against one's own destiny."

"Think!"

Now Ursilla stared silently into the fire. "Charms and herbs, there are none. But when I was a small child, I heard this same great-grandmother whispering to another, the two old ones thinking I was asleep. 'Tis best to burn the sealskin if you're wishing to keep the selchie in human form. But for us, for Marian, this has no meaning. We have nothing. Only the seed, and it cannot be touched, nor should it. Come to bed.''

The two rose. Ursilla took the oil lamp from the table. Together they walked into the little room they had shared for twenty years.

The bell in the church tower had tolled the hour of two. Ursilla lay wakeful and anxious.

Edward sighed and tossed. Suddenly he turned on his side toward her back, and she felt his arm about her waist.

"Ursilla." Edward moved onto his elbow and bent over her face. "Ursilla, do you sleep?"

"No more than you, but stay under the covers. You're letting in an icy blast, shrugged up like that."

Edward put his face against his wife's neck. Her hair smelled of the herbed pillows, and its thickness had warmth.

"Ursilla, I've my mind made up to burn that trunk of yours in the rafters."

Ursilla sat upright, the heavy black locks she loosened at night almost covering her face.

"No! Edward! Burning the few goods I brought with me in marriage!" She pushed her hair from her face. Her voice grew gentle. "And that I have yet to wear. What will this do?"

Edward pulled her down close beside him.

"Think on this. If it be magic—and magic it must be, from what has gone on this week—then the magic of the selchie be as well in that trunk as in the belly of your great-grandmother! Are you following, Ursilla?"

"Aye, Edward."

"Allow it, Ursilla. Allow me to burn the trunk."

Suddenly Ursilla had to shake herself from falling into sleep. Would this not be the least, the least she could do for him?

"Aye." Ursilla turned away from her husband and drew her flannel nightdress close about her. The night *was* bitter cold. Then, as if pulled by a vague memory, a haunting, she added, "Aye, get rid of it, if you must, but don't burn it, Edward. Somehow, I'm troubled by the burning. Perhaps . . . ," and this was said more to herself than Edward, though it was clear by his look he heard, "perhaps you should give it back to the sea."

Chapter 9

LATER THAT MORNING, when Marian had left the house, Edward and Graeme mounted the ladder to the rafters. So much had happened that was alarming, strange for the boy—and now, he and his father were to sink a trunk that his mother had kept in the attic for twenty years! A dread was upon him as he pushed aside the covering board and climbed through the hole onto the narrow beams.

The one window, no more than a slit, was layered with dust and old hanging webs. Graeme used his sleeve to clean off the pane. The trunk stood alone at the far corner.

Father and son dragged it over to the light. It wasn't locked. Inside, neatly folded, were dresses of silk, flounced and sashed and bow trimmed. Un-

derneath were wools, high necked, longsleeved.
There were two pairs of shoes with jet fastenings.
The leather was dry and cracked.

As his father lifted the clothing layer by layer,
Graeme caught sight of a slim gray belt, embroidered with a fine gold-and-silver thread. The boy
reached to touch it.

"Take your hands off!" Edward spoke roughly to his son. "Don't be touching anything in this trunk. I'll do the looking *and* the touching."

"Mother will be miserable, not having these things near her, Father. It's all she has left of her life in the Hebrides, before she came here with you. It's a pity. And Marian could . . ."

"There's already too much left, son. A time to keep, and a time to cast away. Come now"—and Edward let the lid fall shut—"come, catch hold of that handle. Let's be down and into the boat."

It was clumsy work, carrying the swaying object down, down to the ground floor, then through the door. Graeme looked for his mother, but she was nowhere about.

Edward, too, noticed his wife's absence. For him it was a blessing. True, she'd agreed, but he'd enough of her eyes at breakfast.

The rowboat was beached just below the cottage. The descent to it was even steeper than the way to the voe. Years before Edward had chipped out steps, following the rocks' own inclination. Still, it was slow and treacherous with such a burden.

On the strip of beach they tied the trunk with stout cord. At one point Graeme almost cried out but he was mute with a crushing despair. His mother *had* agreed. It was her trunk! He pulled on the cord ends, tightening the knot till his palms burned.

They weighted the stern with a stone anchor and heaved the trunk into the bow of the boat. Then they both sat between the oars. Without a word the two rowed northeast.

The sun shone against the cliffs, glittering with silver mica and pink felsite. Were it not such a mission, the trip would have been a delight for Graeme. He loved to glide close to the rocks, to find the aquamarine in the sea locks and narrow voes and . . .

Edward's voice broke the boy's reveries.

"Head for Busta Stack and we'll dump it just beyond. There's depth there, fathoms."

Fifteen minutes' rowing brought them to the spot. Over the side, the trunk sank almost immediately. Then the stone that weighted the stern.

As they were backfeathering to come about, Graeme saw what looked like a milky crack in the mirrored surface of the water.

"Father! The whale's out there, heading northeast. Out to sea!"

Edward peered into the sun, straining in the direction Graeme pointed.

"I thought it. I knew it, Graeme. Magic so quickly come is as fast gone. Now we can begin a sensible Christian life again, and your sister might even look kindly on one of those fellows who will be coming around this spring. God be praised!"

Edward rowed with quick, short strokes, hardly able to sit on the seat.

Graeme lifted his oar as if it were the weight of the trunk. The sleek white creature that moved in and out of the voe was controlling their lives as with an invisible thread. And sinking the trunk didn't break that thread. No, he, Graeme, didn't understand it, but the whale was to be reckoned with still.

As the boat approached the voe, Graeme sensed instantly that the reckoning had begun.

Marian stood on the rocky ledge, a look of terror on her face. She was pressing the crystal against her lips, and the sounds coming from her were as from a creature mortally wounded. Her skin was as white as the whale, and her eyes had grown double their size. Anguish was all about her.

"What have you done with him?" Each word was uttered as if it would be the last. "If you have killed him . . . I . . ."

Graeme pulled in his oar and jumped onto the land.

"Hush, Marian, hush. Of course we have not killed him. We saw him headed north."

He put an arm around his sister. She fell against his chest and her muffled sobs were as tiny knives into his heart.

"Hush, girl!" The words came harshly from Edward. But such a look did he see on his son's face, a look at once threatening and begging, as to stop his blood. He let the boat drift against the rock.

A noon wind was blowing in from the sea. The sky was gentian and the whitecaps raced each other everywhere on the water. Graeme stood holding his sister.

Sitting in the boat, looking at his two children, Edward was sick with anger. *That creature! On its head a plague!* and without Edward realizing it, the curse escaped him. As the words smote the air, Marian was suddenly quiet. The face she raised to her father was serene; even a bit of color had returned. Her eyes were half closed, the heavy lids low, the black lashes brushing her cheeks. Her dark hair was damp against her face.

"Oh no, Father! You, of all people, must not curse a living creature. Have you not always told us? It is a terrible thing, to damn a life. He is alive. Graeme has just said he is alive. And that is all in this world that matters. Father," Marian looked at

Graeme, then came close to the boat, " 'Cast thy bread upon the waters. For thou shalt find it after many days.' That's from your favorite book. It's all there, you have always told us, it is all there."

Edward stared a moment at his daughter. Then he shoved off toward the tiny beach below the cottage.

"What made you think of that line from the Bible, Marian?" Graeme began climbing back up to the cottage, pulling his sister along.

"When Father cursed, Graeme, it stopped my tears. I feared for Father, cursing. The whale has come to me in joy. Then I heard the words. They're a comfort, aren't they? Such a comfort. I heard the words as if they were a promise. Then I knew he would come back."

The boy kept climbing upward.

"Graeme," Marian's voice was lilting, silken, "when he *does* come back, I shall never leave him. Never!"

Chapter 10

THE WHITE WHALE did not return that day. Nor the next, nor the ones after that. As the weather grew milder, the boats went more often to the far haafbanks and stayed longer. Graeme, heaving line beside his father, wondered what the sea had done with the trunk. And where, in that vast ocean, the white whale was biding time.

She will forget, she will forget. The water lapping the sides of the boat echoed words Graeme longed to believe but which he knew, in the deepest part of his being, were not true.

Ursilla, alone with Marian, watched the empty waters of the voe. *When it comes, may it be swift.* The words became a prayer in Ursilla's heart.

Marian ate little and spoke little.

For the earth, it was a waiting time. The time between late winter and spring, the seed time, between the planting and the growing. The days were misty with sunshine. March melted into April, then May, and there was a green haze upon the land.

The young men of the village gave up their dreams of coming upon Marian among sea pinks and brilliant blue scilla, or beside a burn where pale yellow primroses and bracken lay. Marian stayed by the cottage and slept with a shell against her breast.

Everywhere was airy beauty and no more than surrounding the girl. She was blooming and ripening as the buds swelled and opened on the dog rose beside the door of the cottage.

And then it happened.

Chapter 11

MARIAN HAD risen very early, for now daylight was almost continual. She rode Jo down the cart path to a burnside where the many-headed daisy grew. She wove a small crown for her head and was back at the voe before the sun was much above the watery horizon.

The girl sat down on her stone ledge.

"Today," she whispered to the water. "Today."

The ringed plovers hovered overhead.

"It must have been beautiful, far out at sunset last night." Marian's words hung like dew in the air. "I should have loved to have seen it . . ."

At that moment the blowhole and then the whale's head appeared above the water.

"With you!" the girl cried out, and nearly tripped, scrambling down to the water.

"With you! Oh, you are back!" And her cheeks were flushed as the dawn. "I knew you would return."

She took the circle of daisies from her hair.

"You see, I have a present for you!" And she flung the ringed flowers over his beak. "It's not big enough for your head, I should have thought of that. But it looks handsome, even so. Oh! Where are you going? Please, please . . ."

For the whale had made a strike away from the rocks and gone under.

Marian closed her eyes. *Please, where are you going?*

When she opened her eyes, the white whale's head was again before her. From his mouth hung a belt. It was embroidered with gold thread, yet sleek and smooth and clearly fur. The crown of daisies floated beside him. With one tremendous toss the whale flung the gift toward Marian. She caught it as it hit against her breast.

The girl let the cincture fall over her palms, full length. Water dripped from it in tiny glistening beads.

She felt light as air. "*That* is why you disappeared! I'll have to show Mother and Father and Graeme. I'll have to tell them you're back. Wait! Wait!"

The whale did not move.

Ursilla had just come out the door to pick the few roses already open.

"Mother! See here. Father, Graeme, come look," the girl called breathlessly. Her brother came bounding out. Seeing the cincture, he couldn't move a step. His heart lost beats. He recognized it without doubt. It was the belt that had lain at the bottom of his mother's trunk—the trunk that, weighted and tied, he and his father had sunk off Busta Stack.

"Where did that come from, Marian? Where did you get it? It's Mother's. It was in the trunk . . ."

Marian held the cincture to her cheek and was rubbing it back and forth.

"I don't know what you're talking about, Graeme. He gave it to me. The whale!"

By then Edward was outside. As Marian spoke the last word, her father seized the belt. His face was drained of all color.

"The Lord giveth and the Lord taketh away!" he cried. And suddenly the two were confronting each other, Edward's expression a raging glower, Marian's mouth set and tight. But there was a look in the girl's eyes that caused Edward to fall back next to his wife. "I'll take that, daughter. I'll take that and there will be a roaring peat fire for the selchie and no mistake this time."

"Give it to me, Father." Marian's voice was still breathless, but a vehemence had replaced the joy. "Give it to me, *Father*. He brought it up from the sea. It is mine. You have no right under heaven to take it from me. And what do you mean, selchie? Selchies are seals."

"Give it to her, Edward," Ursilla whispered, and the words were full of pity.

Edward waved the cincture. "This infamy came from your trunk, Ursilla, and now it is here." Turning to his daughter, "You know selchies are human kind turned seal by donning a skin, and this, *I* know, be such a skin!"

Marian looked from her father to her mother and then to Graeme. The boy remembered as if yesterday the last time he stood so, before his father, when Edward's thoughts were on killing the whale. With a shock he recalled what he had been about to say, what he had not said, and what he knew *now* to be the truth of it all.

"Give it to her, Father." Graeme took hold of one end of the belt. It was warm and vibrant. The boy's hand trembled, as did his voice. "*I* beg you, Father. Give Marian what is hers."

Edward had been staring at his daughter as one who looked upon a beloved long gone. Convinced he was on the edge of total loss, the father was trying to trace his daughter's face into his heart—the rounded chin with its delicate cleft, the eyes black as fathoms and set far apart under dark brows. So he stood, with a look that penetrated to the girl's soul. He stood. Then he handed her the belt.

"Oh, Father." Marian came to him. "I thank you. And forgive me. Forgive my anger. I'm not really angry, Father. I'm happy. Be happy also, Father." And she bowed her head as she had done ever since she was a child, to ask his blessing.

Ursilla knew her husband was unable to move. She picked up his hand and laid it upon Marian's head.

Only the pony braying down by the strath broke the stillness. The cloud puffs were bright pink and the sky pale blue, like a sapphire held away from the eye, against the light.

"I'm going back to the water now." Marian took her father's hand from her head and embraced him. She could feel his heart beating madly in his chest. "Father," she smiled radiantly at him, "Father, it will be all right." She stroked his cheek with the ends of her fingers. "Graeme will come with me, won't you, Graeme?"

Graeme looked at his mother. Ursilla had taken her daughter in her arms and was holding her fast.

Marian sought Graeme's hand.

Ursilla and Edward watched their children walk slowly away.

By the time they stood at the sea's edge, tears were spilling over Marian's cheeks, all the while her lips were smiling.

"Graeme?" she asked, looking straight out at the whale. "Will you tie the cincture about my waist? I'll sit down, here." Taking off her shoes, she let her feet skim the water.

"Marian . . ." The boy buried his head in his

sister's neck. Her hair held the spicy odor of the roses. "Marian, how will it be?"

The whale had moved the slightest bit farther out.

"Now . . . please, tie it."

The boy's hands were icy cold and shaking, but he managed to wind the belt around Marian's waist. She watched her brother as if the act were being done to another, not herself.

How will it be? Will I melt away? Will I be whale or seal or sea witch? At this thought Marian ran her fingers over her face, then down her neck and arms and across her breasts. *What will I . . .*

But there was no more time. For, as in a dream when one image imposes itself upon another, Marian Sinclare was soft and gray and velvet as the seal from her waist down. Her body quivered and an exquisite shudder streamed through her.

She raised her arms, drawing Graeme to her. The part of his sister that was sea creature touched his skin. The girl was in ecstasy. The whale was upright, more than half out of the water.

"Graeme, look."

But her brother could not look. He let Marian slip into the water, and as she did so, her cotton blouse floated from her shoulders. The gold chain on which the cross hung and the necklace of pearls had become entwined as one.

Marian swam to the whale, who had lowered himself in the water at the moment she entered it.

"Tell them, Graeme," the girl called. "Tell Mother and Father how it is." She put her face close to the whale's head. "Good-bye, my brother. I shall always be near."

Graeme watched the white whale and Marian swim out to sea. He bent and pulled the blouse out of the water.

"Luck go with you, my sister," he murmured into the air.

THE MERMAID sits upon the rock and smiles. Her home is among the coral in the iridescent depths beneath the waves. Around the rock swims the white whale, magnificent creature. When the longing is upon her, the mermaid swims to a sandy shoal no bigger than herself. There she removes the belt and, steady upon two legs, she climbs the rock stairs to the cottage on the turf. And the white whale moves into the voe to wait, a day, two days, until she again dons the cincture and returns with him to the sea.